⋍⋍ The New Adventures of ⋍⋍
MARY-KATE & ASHLEY ™

The Case Of The
GIGGLING GHOST

Look for more great books in

~ The New Adventures of ~
MARY-KATE & ASHLEY ™

series:

The Case Of The Great Elephant Escape
The Case Of The Summer Camp Caper
The Case Of The Surfing Secret
The Case Of The Green Ghost
The Case Of The Big Scare Mountain Mystery
The Case Of The Slam Dunk Mystery
The Case Of The Rock Star's Secret
The Case Of The Cheerleading Camp Mystery
The Case Of The Flying Phantom
The Case Of The Creepy Castle
The Case Of The Golden Slipper
The Case Of The Flapper 'Napper
The Case Of The High Seas Secret
The Case Of The Logical I Ranch
The Case Of The Dog Camp Mystery
The Case Of The Screaming Scarecrow
The Case Of The Jingle Bell Jinx
The Case Of The Game Show Mystery
The Case Of The Mall Mystery
The Case Of The Weird Science Mystery
The Case Of Camp Crooked Lake
The Case Of The Giggling Ghost

and coming soon
The Case Of The Candy Cane Clue

Look for more great books in

The New Adventures of
MARY-KATE & ASHLEY™

The Case Of The
GIGGLING GHOST

by Melinda Metz

HarperEntertainment
An Imprint of HarperCollins*Publishers*

A PARACHUTE PRESS BOOK

PARACHUTE PRESS

Parachute Publishing, L.L.C.
156 Fifth Avenue
New York, NY 10010

 DUALSTAR PUBLICATIONS

Dualstar Publications
c/o Thorne and Company
A Professional Law Corporation
1801 Century Park East
Los Angeles, CA 90067

▦HarperEntertainment

An Imprint of HarperCollins*Publishers*
10 East 53rd Street, New York, NY 10022

First printing: September 2002

Printed in the United States of America

SCAREDY CAT!

"**M**ary-Kate? Ashley? Want to see something really creepy inside my backpack?" my friend Patty O'Leary asked.

Patty turned in her bus seat and opened the zipper on her pack a tiny bit.

"What do you think?" I asked my twin sister, Ashley. "Should we look?"

Ashley grinned. "It's only three days till Halloween. Why not?"

"What about you, Rachel?" Patty said to the girl sitting next to her. "Want to see what's inside my backpack? Or are you too chicken?"

Rachel's brown eyes opened wide. She bit her bottom lip. "I-I'm not chicken," she told Patty.

I tried not to laugh. Everyone in our class knew that Rachel hated monsters and ghosts and hearing creepy stories—especially around Halloween.

"Okaaaay," Patty said. "But don't say I didn't warn you!" Slowly, Patty unzipped her backpack the rest of the way.

Rachel peered into the opening. "There's nothing in there," she announced.

Ashley and I leaned over Rachel's shoulder. I didn't see anything either.

"It's way at the bottom," Patty whispered. "Look closer."

Rachel dipped her head lower. Her long, black ponytail fell in front of her face.

Then Eric Kramer reached over from his seat across the aisle. He jabbed his finger into Rachel's side. "Boo!" he shouted out.

"Yaaaaaaah!" Rachel let out a scream.

Patty and Eric laughed like crazy.

"We scared Rachel *again*!" Patty cried.

Eric slapped Patty a high five. "That's the second time this afternoon!"

"I still can't believe we scared her with that stupid Jell-O she brought to the class Halloween party today." Patty laughed. "I mean, who gets scared by grape Jell-O?"

"Why don't you two just leave Rachel alone?" I said. "It could happen to anybody!" Well, maybe it couldn't, but Princess Patty and Eric didn't have to embarrass Rachel that way.

Rachel's face turned a deep red—almost as red as Patty's hair. Then she gave me a small smile. "Thanks," she whispered.

I glanced out the bus window. "Hey, everybody, check it out. You can see the top of the Ferris wheel from here!"

Ashley leaned across me. "Excellent! I

can't believe it's finally the opening day of the Halloween Carnival."

Lots of kids from our fifth-grade class had volunteered to work at the first-ever Halloween carnival in our town. The carnival was scheduled to open today, Thursday, and run through to Sunday, which was Halloween!

Patty and Eric were in charge of the win-a-goldfish game. Rachel, Ashley, our friend Tim Park, and I were in charge of the ring toss.

We had spent all of yesterday afternoon at the fair grounds, putting the finishing touches on our booths. Now everything was ready to go!

"Our game booth is going to be great," I said. "And it's going to score tons of money for the animals!"

Besides being major fun, the carnival was raising money to help the Furry Friends Animal Shelter.

Tim turned in the seat in front of me. "I practiced my intro for about a million hours last night," he announced. He cleared his throat. "Step right up, ladies and gentlemen, and try your luck at the ring toss! We've got the coolest prizes—"

"No way!" Eric interrupted. "Patty and I have the coolest prizes. At our booth you can win real live goldfish. Right, Patty?"

"That's right," Patty answered. "My dad delivered the goldfish to our booth this morning. He said they were the best prizes anywhere."

Ashley rolled her eyes. I knew what she was thinking. Patty *loved* to brag. And her dad bought her anything she wanted. That was why we called her Princess Patty.

The bus stopped at the gate to the carnival parking lot. I jumped to my feet. "Let's go! This is our stop!"

We stepped off the bus. And we were greeted with the sound of shouting voices.

"Who's yelling like that?" I asked.

"It's coming from the carnival entrance," Tim added.

"What's happening?" Rachel asked.

"Let's find out!" Ashley said. "Come on!"

We all took off across the parking lot. At the carnival entrance, we found about ten people marching in a circle.

"Stop the Halloween carnival! Stop the Halloween carnival!" the people chanted.

"Huh? Why would anyone want to stop the carnival?" Eric asked me.

I shrugged. I had no idea.

"Hey, you," one of the marchers shouted to us. "Go away! You shouldn't be here!"

I gazed up at the marcher. He was tall, skinny, bald—and he had a big wet spot on the front of his shirt. He held a giant-size hot dog in his left hand.

"But we're *supposed* to be here," Tim explained. "We're working at game booths in the carnival."

The man took a bite of his hot dog. A glob of mustard dripped out of the bun and landed on his shoe. Yuck!

"Don't worry, there aren't going to be game booths," the man told us.

"What do you mean?" I asked. "Why not?"

The man folded his arms across his chest. "Because there isn't going to be a Halloween carnival!"

STOP THE CARNIVAL!

"**T**here isn't going to be a carnival? Says who?" Patty demanded.

The man handed each of us a sheet of paper. "I'm Byron Adams," he said. "That flyer I gave you has all the information you need."

I read the first line on the piece of paper. It said, "Join our fight! Become a member of OOH!"

"OOH?" I asked. "What's that?"

"It's the name of my group," Byron

replied. "It stands for Organization Opposed to Halloween."

"What's wrong with Halloween?" Ashley asked.

"Halloween is noisy," Byron said. "It involves a lot of candy, which means a lot of sugar. Sugar is bad for your teeth. Plus it gives children nightmares." He flicked his hot dog toward us with each point he made. I had to duck to avoid flying drops of mustard.

"But all the money the carnival makes will go to the Furry Friends animal shelter," I told Byron. "If you close the carnival, what will happen to the shelter?"

Byron shrugged. "I don't care. Twenty people have already signed my petition to shut down the carnival. This place will be closed before Halloween."

"No way!" Tim argued. "We worked hard on our booths and we're not going anywhere." He walked right past the group of chanting OOH members and through the carnival entrance. We all followed him inside.

"That guy doesn't know what he's talking about," Eric said. "The carnival is *definitely* going to open. Look—they're testing the Ferris wheel right now!"

"And all the food booths are getting ready," Tim added. He sniffed the air. "I can smell the cotton candy—and the hot dogs—and the pizza."

I laughed. Tim loves food. He has the biggest appetite of anyone in our school!

"What are we all standing around here for? Patty asked. "We have to get ready for our customers!"

"Let's go!" Ashley and I cheered.

Our booth was between a Sno-cone stand and Princess Patty's and Eric's goldfish stand.

"Hey, guys! Over here!" We turned and saw Rachel's cousin, Billy, a few feet from our booths. He was leaning against a fortune-telling machine.

We had met Billy a bunch of times before. He was sixteen years old, and he had black hair and brown eyes just like Rachel.

Billy was working at the carnival, too. And he had the best job of all. Billy was in charge of the haunted house!

"There's some scary stuff going on around here," Billy said as we walked up to him. He lowered his voice. "Don't tell anyone, but I think my haunted house is really haunted."

"That's ridiculous," Patty said.

"Don't you believe in ghosts?" Billy asked.

Patty laughed. "Nope."

"There are no such things as ghosts," Eric said. "Everyone knows that—except Rachel!"

"Come into my haunted house," Billy said. "Then you'll believe." He wiggled his eyebrows. "You *will* believe!"

"Nice act," I said. "I bet you'll raise a lot of money for the animal shelter."

"I hope so," Billy replied. He glanced at his watch. "Gotta go. I have to put up the cobwebs!" Billy waved to us as he jogged off toward the haunted house.

Rachel stared into the glass booth of the fortune-telling machine. A statue of an old gypsy woman sat behind a wooden table. A deck of cards was spread out before her.

"I want to get my fortune told." Rachel shivered. "But it looks too creepy."

"I'll do it," Patty said, nudging Rachel aside. She dropped a quarter into the slot. The old woman's eyes began to glow. She waved her hand over the cards and a fortune fell into the tray at the bottom of the machine.

Patty picked up the card and read it out loud. "'Those who do not fear ghosts now, will fear them soon.' Signed 'The Giggling Ghost.'"

"How weird," Eric whispered. "It's as if someone just heard us saying we didn't believe in..." His voice trailed off.

At that moment, someone started to giggle. "Hee-hee-hee-hee-heeee!"

The sound was high-pitched and kind of whispery, but loud enough for all of us to hear. It was so creepy it gave me a prickly feeling on the back of my neck. I glanced around the group. Who was laughing like that?

It wasn't Ashley. It wasn't Patty or Eric. It wasn't Tim or Rachel. And it wasn't coming from the fortune-telling machine.

So who was it?

3

THE FORTUNE TELLER

"*Hee-hee-hee-hee-heeee!*" The giggling grew louder, then faded away.

"Was that...the Giggling Ghost?" Tim asked.

"Maybe Billy wasn't kidding," Rachel said. Her voice quivered. "Maybe there *is* a ghost at the carnival."

Ashley shook her head. "No way," she said. "Eric's right. Ghosts aren't real. There must be some other explanation."

I wasn't surprised that Ashley had said

that. My sister is very logical. Much more than I am.

Ashley and I look a lot alike. We both have shoulder-length blond hair and blue eyes. But inside we're totally different. I like to trust my gut feelings. Ashley thinks carefully about *everything*. But that's why we make great partners.

Ashley and I are detectives. We run the Olsen and Olsen Detective Agency from the attic of our house. Our basset hound, Clue, is our silent partner.

"Can I see the fortune?" Ashley asked. She took the card from Patty and studied it. I stared at it over her shoulder.

The fortune was written on an old-looking, yellowed piece of paper. The message was in script handwriting, with lots of curls and swirls at the ends of all the letters.

"Let's go find the person in charge of the fortune-telling machine," Ashley said. "Maybe she can explain the weird fortune to us."

A few booths away, I spotted a teenage girl sitting behind a folding table. She had bouncy brown hair and shiny pink lips. The sign in front of her table said INFORMATION.

"Excuse me," I called to the girl. "Can you tell us where to find the person running the fortune-telling machine?"

"You found her," the girl replied. "My name is Daisy Fuller."

"We're carnival volunteers, too," I said. I introduced myself, Ashley, and our friends to Daisy.

"We need to ask you a few questions about this fortune." Ashley held the card out to Daisy.

Daisy looked at the weird fortune and frowned. "This isn't one of the official cards," she announced.

"What do you mean?" I asked.

"I put the fortune cards into that machine half an hour ago," Daisy reported. "And they don't look anything like this."

"So who put *this* fortune into the machine?" I asked.

"I have no idea," Daisy admitted.

Ashley pulled her detective notebook from her backpack. "Something weird is going on here," she said.

"Right." I nodded. "If nobody knows who put the creepy card into the machine, then we have a mystery to solve!"

4

A GIGGLING GHOST?

"**H**ave you ever heard of the Giggling Ghost?" I asked Daisy.

"No, but I'm a ghost expert," Daisy replied. "Well, at least I *want* to be. I'm taking a class at my college that's all about ghosts."

"You can study ghosts at college?" Ashley asked.

Daisy nodded. "One of the first things we learned is that ghosts usually appear because they have unfinished business to take care of. Or they're angry about something."

"See!" Rachel burst out. "Patty and Eric said they didn't believe in ghosts, and the ghost heard them. They made it angry." She turned to Daisy. "We heard the ghost giggle!"

"But there are no such things as ghosts," Ashley and I said at the same time.

"Yeah. Ghosts aren't real," Tim agreed.

"Well, if ghosts aren't real, then *who* was giggling?" Daisy asked.

Nobody answered. Nobody *could* answer. Because none of us knew where that giggling had come from.

Ashley glanced at her watch. "It's getting late. Come on, everyone. We have to get our booths set up before the carnival opens."

"Thanks, Daisy!" I called as we walked away from her table.

"No problem," Daisy said. "And if the ghost comes back, be sure to let me know, okay? I'm writing a paper for my ghost

class. I'll get an A for sure if I can put in details about a real live ghost!"

Patty and Eric were quiet while we headed to our booths. I wondered if they were thinking about the Giggling Ghost.

Patty finally spoke. "Wow! Your booth looks great!" she exclaimed.

I smiled. Our booth did look great. It was made of wood that was painted bright yellow. It was square-shaped, with a red and yellow counter on every side. Ashley, Rachel, Tim, and I would each have a counter to stand behind.

"I call the side closest to the food," Tim yelled. "I want to smell those goodies the whole time I'm working!"

Ashley picked the side facing the haunted house. Rachel's side had a view of Eric and Patty's booth. My side faced the fortune-telling machine.

Patty and Eric left for their booth. I glanced around and noticed that a few

people were already coming into the carnival. We had to set up fast.

"We need some rings on each side of the booth," Ashley decided. She grabbed a stack of plastic rings from a shelf beneath the counter. The stuffed animals we brought as prizes were stored under there, too.

"We should all have change in our apron pockets," I added. "Let's—"

I was interrupted by a loud scream.

"Oh, no!" Ashley exclaimed. "That's Patty!"

5

THE HAUNTED HOUSE

"**N**oooo!" Patty screamed again. "My fish! My fish!"

We all raced to Patty and Eric's booth. The shelves on the wall of the booth were filled with goldfish bowls.

Every bowl held a goldfish. And every single goldfish was absolutely still.

"Oh, no!" I whispered to Ashley. "Those fish don't look alive."

Eric paced back and forth. "Who could have done this to our fish?" he asked.

Ashley peered into the closest fishbowl. Then she reached into the water and pulled out the goldfish.

"Eww!" I cried. "What are you doing?"

"These fish aren't real," Ashley said. "They're plastic!"

"Plastic? But that's impossible!" Patty burst out. "My dad brought real goldfish to our booth this morning!"

I studied the fishbowls. "Ashley is right," I reported. "Someone switched your fish."

Then I noticed something else. Something weird. There was purple goo smeared all over the fishbowls.

I picked up one bowl, careful not to the get any gunk on my fingers. "What is this stuff?" I wondered aloud.

"*Hee-hee-hee-hee-hee-hee!*" There it was again. The whispery giggling!

Rachel gave me a frightened look. "What if that goo is from the ghost?" she said. "What if the ghost took Patty and Eric's fish—and left this…this yucky *ghost slime*?"

"Or maybe whoever took the fish wants us to *believe* there's a ghost," Ashley said.

"Let's take a sample of it—whatever it is," I suggested.

"Here." Eric handed me a plastic container. "We were going to keep our money in this, but we'll find something else."

"Thanks," I replied. I held the container up to a fishbowl and Ashley used a pen to scrape some of the purple goo into it.

"What about our fish?" Patty whined. "We have to find them!"

"Patty's right," I said. "But where should we start?"

"How about the haunted house?" Rachel suggested. "I bet that's the first place a ghost would hide."

"Good idea, Rachel," I said.

"And if Billy is there, we can ask him if he saw anything strange," Ashley said.

I handed Tim the plastic container with

our goo clue inside. "Can you put this on the shelf below the counter in our booth? I want to make sure it stays safe," I said.

"Okay," Tim said. Then Ashley and I ran to the haunted house.

When we got there, we told Billy everything that had happened. He said he hadn't seen anything unusual. But he turned on all the lights inside the haunted house so that we could look around.

"Ready?" Ashley asked, staring up at the gray, broken-down building.

"Ready," I answered.

We took a step forward. *Crreeeeaaak!* The door to the haunted house opened slowly—all by itself! Ashley and I walked inside.

WHAM! I jumped when the door slammed shut behind us.

We crept down a long, narrow hallway. A row of painted pictures lined the walls on either side.

As we moved forward, I stared up at the paintings. Each one was of a person dressed in old-fashioned clothes.

I gasped when I looked at the eyes of the people in the paintings—they seemed to follow me wherever I went!

"I didn't think this place would be so scary with the lights on," I whispered. "But it is."

"I know." Ashley moved closer to me.

At the end of the hall was a long, narrow staircase. Spiderwebs hung from the banister. "I guess we have to go up there," I whispered.

"Yup," Ashley agreed.

Together, we tiptoed up the stairs.

Everything in the haunted house was quiet. So quiet, I could hear my heart pounding in my chest.

At the top of the staircase we saw a huge door. I glanced down at the door handle. It was in the shape of a bat's wing.

I grabbed the handle and pushed open the door.

"It's a dining room," Ashley said as we stepped inside. "And look what's for dinner!"

She pointed at the long table. Sitting in the center was a large platter. And on the platter was a human head!

"It's fake. It's totally fake," Ashley said as we moved closer to the table.

Then the eyes of the head snapped open. "Will you be joining us for dinner?" the head asked.

"Aaaah!" Ashley jumped back. She crashed into me and I fell onto the floor.

Two hands came down on my shoulders and pulled me to my feet. "Thanks, Ashl—"

Wait a minute. Ashley was standing in front of me. Whoever picked me up was behind me.

"Oh, no!" I cried. "It's the ghost!"

6

THE GOO IS GONE!

"Where? Where is the ghost? I want to see it!" a voice shouted.

I spun around and saw Daisy, the girl from the information booth. I breathed a sigh of relief. "What are you doing here?"

Daisy wound one of her brown curls around her finger. "I couldn't stop thinking about that ghost. I know I'll get an A on my paper if I can see it. I asked your friends, and they told me where you were. So I decided to tag along."

"Will you be joining us for dinner?" the mechanical head on the platter asked again. It grinned, showing a mouth full of pointed teeth.

"No, we won't!" Ashley shouted at the head. "Come on," she said to Daisy and me. "We have to find those fish."

We searched the entire dining room, but we didn't find anything. Ashley pointed to two doors that led out of the room. "Which way do we go now?" she asked.

"Left is lucky," I answered. I opened the door to the left and stepped through.

"Maybe not so lucky," I mumbled. The three of us were standing in a cemetery!

Stars had been painted on the ceiling of the room so it looked like the night sky. Rows of tombstones were stuck into piles of dirt. Everything looked totally real.

There were more mounds of dirt in front of each tombstone—as if something had just been buried there.

"There are lots of places in here to hide the fish," Ashley said. "Let's check behind all the tombstones."

She marched over to the closest grave and peeked behind the tombstone. Then she moved on.

I headed toward the other end of the room and started searching.

"Hey, does it feel cold in here to you?" Daisy asked me. "My professor told us it gets cold when ghosts are around."

"It is a *little* cold," I said. But that didn't mean a ghost was there, I told myself. Right?

"Mary-Kate! Daisy! Come over here," Ashley called out.

Daisy and I found Ashley standing by a coffin next to an open grave.

"Doesn't this look like a great hiding place?" she asked. She tapped the coffin that sat next to the big hole. "Help me open it, okay?"

A shiver ran down my spine. I grabbed one end of the coffin lid. Ashley took the other.

Squeeeeek! The coffin lid shrieked as we pulled it open.

Ashley looked inside—and gasped.

"What is it?" I leaped away.

Ashley reached in an pulled out a small fish tank loaded with goldfish. "They're here," Ashley cheered. "We found the fish!"

"Let's get this back to the booth right away!" I said.

"I'll carry it for you," Daisy volunteered. "That tank looks heavy." She took the tank from Ashley. Water sloshed over the side. "Eww! I got fish water all over my shirt," she complained.

I looked over at her. Yep. She had a big wet splotch on the front of her pink shirt.

"Hey, look at this! I found another clue!" Ashley said. She reached down to the bottom of the coffin and pulled out a pizza crust. "Whoever hid the fish here probably left this crust behind."

I grinned. "We should show this to Rachel. It's proof that there's no ghost."

"Right," Ashley agreed. "Because everyone knows that ghosts don't eat pizza!"

"That's true," Daisy admitted. "Ghosts don't eat food. But they do leave behind something called ectoplasm."

"What's that?" I asked.

"There's some right there." Daisy pointed to the side of the coffin. Smeared across the wood, was the same purple goo I found on Patty's fishbowls.

"That slime is proof that a ghost *was* here," Daisy said. "It was probably standing right where we are now!"

"We have a sample of that goo," Ashley told her. "We'll examine it when we get home tonight. But right now we have to get back to our booth."

We left the haunted house as quickly as we

could. Daisy delivered the fish to Patty and Eric. Ashley and I returned to the ring toss.

"Tim, where did you put our container of goo?" I asked. I wanted to stick the ectoplasm—or whatever it was—into my backpack. It was a very important clue.

"It's on the shelf, next to the prizes," Tim answered.

I bent down to look at the shelf. The container wasn't there. "Are you sure this is where you put it?" I called.

"Double sure," Tim told me.

I checked underneath the prizes. No container. I checked on all the other shelves. The container wasn't there, either.

"Oh, no," I moaned. Our very important clue was gone!

NAMING THE SUSPECTS

Ashley flipped open her detective notebook. While Rachel and Tim watched the booth, we walked over to a quiet corner.

"I think it's time to make a list of suspects," she said. "We need to figure out who wants us to think there is a ghost here."

"Hey!" I snapped my fingers. "What about Byron Adams?"

"Byron Adams?" Ashley repeated. "Why him?"

"Well, he and OOH want to close the

carnival. People might not want to come here if they think there is a real ghost around!" I said.

"Good thinking, Mary-Kate," Ashley said. She wrote "Suspect #1: Byron Adams" in her detective notebook.

"And hey! Remember that big wet spot on Byron's shirt?" I asked. "Daisy got one exactly like it when she picked up the tank of goldfish. That *must* mean Byron is the one who took the fish!"

Ashley tapped her lip with the end of her pen. "Interesting," she said.

"It's more than interesting, Ashley," I said. "It's the answer! Byron's got to be our man. This case is closed—and in record time!" I lifted my hand for a high five. But Ashley didn't slap it.

"Byron *could* have gotten his shirt wet when he stole the fish," she told me. "But maybe there's another explanation."

I sighed and let my hand drop to my

side. I knew exactly what Ashley was going to say next. It was what she always said when I jumped to conclusions.

"We need more proof," Ashley told me.

"I know, I know," I groaned.

"Let's think about *all* the things the ghost did," Ashley suggested. "That might help us come up with other suspects."

I counted out the ghost events on my fingers. "He put a creepy fortune in the fortune-telling machine," I said. "He swiped Patty and Eric's fish and hid them in the haunted house. And he smeared purple goo all over the fishbowls and the coffin."

"Byron could have done those things," Ashley admitted. "He was at the gates before we even got to the carnival."

"Which means he could have sneaked inside and planted that creepy message," I said, picking up Ashley's thought. "Then he could have stolen Patty's fish, and hidden them inside the haunted house!"

"Who else could have done all those things?" Ashley asked.

I thought and thought. "How about Daisy?" I suggested.

"Daisy?" Ashley asked. "But she seemed really nice. Why would she want to wreck the carnival?"

"She said she would get an A on her paper if she saw a real ghost, remember?" I explained.

"Uh-huh." Ashley nodded.

"So maybe she created the fake ghost so she could use it for her homework!" I guessed.

"Sister, you are one smart detective!" Ashley said. She wrote "Suspect #2: Daisy Fuller" in her notebook.

"Daisy told us herself that she loaded the fortune-telling machine. She could have switched the real cards for the Giggling Ghost one easily," I pointed out.

"Plus, since she works here, she could

have gotten to the carnival early, grabbed the fish, and hid them in the haunted house," Ashley finished. "This is great, Mary-Kate! We have two strong suspects."

"But wait a minute. We're forgetting something," I pointed out. "Something very important."

"What's that?" Ashley asked.

"The giggling," I answered. "Who could have made that creepy giggling sound?" I bit my bottom lip. "Looks like we have one more suspect to write down."

"Who?" Ashley asked.

I gulped. "The Giggling Ghost!"

8

A CRUSTY CLUE

"**S**tep right up and win a prize!" I shouted. "Try your luck at the ring toss!"

It was Friday afternoon. Tim, Ashley, Rachel, and I were in our booth, trying to make some money for the animal shelter.

Ashley sighed and leaned against her counter in the ring-toss booth. "I was hoping there would be more people today, since Halloween is only two days away," she said.

"We've been open for hours," Tim said,

"and Rachel and I have made only four dollars."

"This is awful," Rachel added. "All this work for nothing."

"Hey, guys!" Patty hurried up to our booth. "You have to read this!" She shoved a newspaper into Ashley's hands.

"Patty, how much money have you and Eric made at your booth today?" Tim asked.

"Almost none," Patty answered. "And this article is why." She pointed at the newspaper.

"What's it about?" Tim asked.

"The article says that the haunted house at the carnival is really haunted," Ashley answered.

Rachel stared at us, her eyes wide. "I knew it," she whispered.

"And there's a quote from Daisy that says she saw proof," Ashley continued. "The newspaper calls her a ghost expert."

"A ghost expert, huh?" I repeated. "I wonder if the teacher grading her paper will read that article."

"If he does, Daisy will definitely get an A," Tim added. "You can't flunk an expert."

"Byron is quoted in the article, too," Ashley reported. "He says the carnival should be shut down immediately if there's a chance that it's haunted."

"Big surprise," Tim muttered. "So now that we know why no one is here, what do we do about it?"

"The carnival is bound to be the most crowded on Halloween night," Ashley reminded us. "If we figure out who the ghost is before then, we'll still get tons of customers. And we'll make lots of money for charity."

"But Halloween is only two days away." Patty crossed her arms. She looked from me to Ashley. "Do you really think you can solve the case in time?"

"Of course," I said. But I saw a little wrinkle form between Ashley's eyebrows. I knew she was worried.

"Come on, Ashley," I said. "Let's get to work. I say we pay a visit to Daisy."

We waved good-bye to Rachel, Tim, and Patty. Then we headed for the fortune-telling machine.

"Look out!" I cried. I pulled Ashley out of the way of a teenage guy, carrying a stack of pizza boxes. The boxes were piled so high that he couldn't see her.

"Ooops. Sorry," the guy mumbled.

"Wow! Somebody sure likes pizza," I said.

"Yeah. It's for the people protesting outside. I can't believe that I have to bring them pizza!" He used his chin to keep the tower of boxes steady.

"You mean the people from OOH?" Ashley asked.

"That's right," the pizza guy answered.

"And you won't believe this. The leader—that guy Byron—he hates pizza crust. So today he made me cut all the crusts off."

I gave Ashley's hand a little squeeze. Byron didn't like pizza crusts! And we found a pizza crust in the haunted house near the missing fish!

The pizza guy sighed. "Well, I'd better deliver these while they're still hot. See you later."

As he walked away, Ashley jotted down a note in her detective book. "Byron hates pizza crust. Just like our ghost."

We walked over to the fortune-telling machine and peeked around the side. From there, we could see Daisy sitting at her folding table, reading from a big textbook. The title on the front of the book was written in big, orange letters: BOO: A HISTORY OF REAL AMERICAN GHOST STORIES.

For a few moments Daisy did nothing but flip the pages in her book. But then, I saw her lift something to her mouth—a slice of pizza!

She took a last bite of the pizza and tossed the crust into the garbage.

I grabbed Ashley by the arm. "Did you see that?" I whispered. "Daisy could be the one who left that pizza crust in the coffin. It looks like she hates crust as much as Byron does."

"Let's talk to her," Ashley suggested. "I have a couple of questions I want to ask. Maybe we can get a few clues out of her."

"Good idea," I said. We walked toward Daisy's table. "Hi, Daisy!" I called.

She looked up from her book. "Hi, what's up? Have you found any more ectoplasm?"

Ashley shook her head. "Nope. And we even lost the sample we had," she admitted.

"That's too bad," Daisy said. "I was hoping I could borrow it. I wanted to show it to my ghost class tomorrow."

"Do you think you could show us how

the fortune-telling machine works?" Ashley asked. "It's kind of important."

"Sure," Daisy answered. "Follow me." She smoothed down her curly hair, then led us to the fortune-telling machine. There was a small door in the back. Daisy swung it open.

I noticed she didn't need a key or anything. That meant any of our suspects could have slipped the ghost fortune into the machine.

"All you do is take a stack of cards and load them into that slot," Daisy explained. "Then this lever slides out one card every time someone puts in a quarter."

"And those are the official cards?" Ashley asked.

"Uh-huh." Daisy pulled one out and handed it to Ashley.

"'You will meet a handsome stranger,'" Ashley read aloud. Then she showed me the card.

"These cards aren't handwritten like the Giggling Ghost's card," I noticed. "They're printed by a machine."

"Yeah. We stack hundreds of fortunes in this thing," Daisy answered. "That would be too many to write by hand."

"Well, we should get back to our booth," Ashley said. "But before we go, could I get an autograph?"

"From me?" Daisy asked. She sounded surprised.

I was surprised too. Why would Ashley want Daisy's autograph?

"Of course," Ashley said. She pulled out the newspaper article Patty gave her—the one with the quote from Daisy. "See? You're famous now!"

Daisy blushed. "Well, I wouldn't say *famous...*"

Ashley handed her a pen. Daisy signed her name in big, round letters.

"Thanks, Daisy. Come on, Mary-Kate."

Ashley grabbed my sleeve and pulled me away from the fortune-telling machine.

"What was that about?" I asked.

Ashley waved the newspaper article in my face. "Think about it!" she said. "The ghost card was handwritten by someone. And now we have a copy of Daisy's handwriting. If the two match, we just solved this case!"

9

A PERFECT MATCH

"**W**ell, what are we waiting for?" I asked Ashley. "Let's take out that fortune!" I opened my backpack and took out the Giggling Ghost's fortune card.

Ashley held up Daisy's signature next to the card—and sighed. "Well, our case *isn't* solved! Daisy's handwriting doesn't match the handwriting on the card at all."

"So *she* can't be our ghost," I said. "But the handwriting on the card is the perfect way to find out who our ghost really is."

"Let's get a sample from Byron right away!" Ashley said.

We headed straight for the main gates of the fairground.

"No more Halloween!" I heard the OOH people shouting. "Close the carnival now!"

"There's Byron." Ashley pointed him out, and we hurried over.

"What are you kids doing here?" he asked.

"We've been thinking about Halloween," I yelled over the chanting. "About how noisy it is and everything."

"That's right," Ashley hollered. "So we wanted to sign your petition. Could we see it?"

"Of course!" Byron shouted back. He pulled a sheet of paper out of his pocket. He unfolded it and handed it to Ashley.

"Thanks!" Ashley yelled. "We'll just take it somewhere a little quieter."

"We'll bring it right back," I added.

"Fine," Byron answered. "I need pizza!" he cried.

One of the OOH members trotted up and handed Byron a slice of pizza. No crust. He took a bite. A blob of cheese slid down his chin. Yuck! He was really messy!

Ashley and I moved far enough away from Byron's group to talk to each other without screaming.

I pulled out the fortune-telling card again. Ashley and I looked from the handwriting on the card to Byron's signature. It was the first one on the very top of the list.

"Rats! Byron's signature definitely doesn't match," I said. "He's not a good suspect anymore either."

"Let's check the rest of the petition," Ashley suggested. "Maybe someone else's handwriting matches the ghost's."

Together, we scanned the list. "Nope, nope," I muttered. "Nope, nope, nope."

"No handwriting matches," Ashley admitted. "That means we're totally out of suspects!"

We flopped down on a nearby bench.

"Ashley, I know we don't believe in ghosts, but is there any way that Rachel could be right? Could there really be a ghost haunting this carnival?" I asked.

"I'm telling you, Mary-Kate, there has to be another answer—another suspect that we haven't come up with yet," Ashley replied. "Think carefully. Who else would want to scare people by making them believe that the carnival is haunted?"

I pressed my lips together. *Who would want to scare people?* I wondered.

I gasped when I came up with an answer. "What about Patty and Eric?" I asked. "They're always trying to scare Rachel. Convincing her that the carnival is haunted would be the biggest scare ever!"

"They wouldn't ruin the carnival just to play a joke on Rachel," Ashley said, "would they?"

Just thinking about that made me feel

sick. "I hope not," I answered. "But they could have hidden their fish. And they could have put the ghost card into the fortune-telling machine."

"The only thing we can't explain right now is the giggling," Ashley said. "But except for that, Patty and Eric are really good suspects."

"Come on. Let's go over to the goldfish booth," I said.

"Right. We need to get handwriting samples from Eric and Patty," Ashley agreed.

We rushed back to Byron. "Thanks for letting us look at this," I told him. I handed him back the petition.

Byron put it in his pocket. "Water!" he shouted out.

One of the OOH members threw him a sports bottle full of water. Byron pulled off the top and took a long, long drink. Water dribbled down his chin and onto his shirt. It made a big wet spot.

"That's probably how he got the wet spot on his shirt the other day," Ashley said.

"Yeah," I said. "He's always spilling something on himself."

Ashley and I raced to the goldfish booth.

"There's our handwriting sample," I whispered. I nodded toward the big sign Eric and Patty had made for their goldfish booth. It said WIN A REAL, LIVE GOLDFISH. ONLY $1.

Ashley pulled the Giggling Ghost fortune out of her pocket. "The 'g' in 'goldfish' doesn't look anything like the 'g's on the Giggling Ghost fortune," Ashley said. "Whoever wrote that sign is cleared."

"Hi, guys!" I said, walking up to Patty and Eric. "I didn't notice it before, but your sign is really cool. Which one of you guys made it?"

"I did the writing. Patty drew the fish," Eric answered.

"I wanted to do the writing too," Patty told us. "I can write lots of different ways.

But Eric said it wasn't fair for me to draw *and* do the writing."

"Can you really write in different ways?" I asked.

Patty grabbed a piece of paper and a marker. "Watch this." She wrote the words "win a goldfish" with lots of curlicues. Then with no curlicues at all. She wrote the "g"s so they looked like snakes. Then she wrote them so they looked like smiling faces.

"That's amazing, Patty!" I exclaimed.

None of Patty's handwriting styles matched the Giggling Ghost fortune card exactly, but Patty *had* said she could write lots of different ways.

I glanced at Ashley. I knew she was thinking the same thing I was. Patty was now our number one suspect.

"Hey, Patty," Ashley said. "Want to go over to the pizza booth and get a slice?"

I tried not to smile. I knew exactly what Ashley was up to. She wanted to find out whether or not Patty liked the crust on her pizza.

"Sure," Patty answered.

"Bring me back one with pepperoni," Eric called as we left.

"What kind are you going to get?" I asked Patty when we reached the booth.

"Black olives. A square slice without the crust," Patty said.

"We've got her!" I whispered to Ashley. "Patty is the ghost!"

THE GHOST STRIKES AGAIN

After we finished our pizza, we headed back to our booth. Ashley leaned on the counter and drummed her fingers on the wood surface. "Patty is a really strong suspect," she said. "But lots of people don't like pizza crust. We need more evidence against her."

"What do you think we should do next?" I asked.

"I can only think of one thing—go back into the haunted house," Ashley announced.

"Yeah. Maybe our ghost left another clue behind. One that we missed before," I agreed. "But we'd better hurry. The carnival will be closing soon."

"We're going to the haunted house," I told Rachel and Tim. "Be back soon."

"Wait! I want to come, too," Tim volunteered. He turned to Rachel. "If it's okay with you."

"I wouldn't go into that house for a million dollars," Rachel answered. "But you go ahead. I'll start shutting down the booth."

I turned to leave and spotted something lying on the ground. It was a key chain with a small black box attached to it.

"Hey! Look what I found." I picked up the key chain and turned it over in my hand. I noticed a big red button in the center of the box. Something about it looked very familiar to me.

"Oh, that's mine," Rachel said. "I must have dropped it." She took the key chain and shoved it into the pocket of her jeans. "Thanks, Mary-Kate."

"No problem," I answered. "We'll be right back." Ashley, Tim, and I raced toward the haunted house.

"Hey! Where are you guys going?" Eric yelled as we ran by the goldfish booth.

"Haunted house," I answered without stopping.

"I'm coming with you!" Eric called. He climbed over the counter of his booth, leaving Patty to close up.

We all ran as fast as we could. But when we reached the entrance to the haunted house, Rachel's cousin Billy was putting out the Closed sign.

Tim checked his watch. "Hey, no fair. There's still a whole minute left before the carnival closes!" he protested.

Billy laughed. "Okay. You four can be my last customers of the night." He opened the front door to the house.

"Thanks, Billy." Ashley said. The four of us stepped into the front hallway.

WHAM! The door slammed shut behind us. I gulped when I realized that this time Billy hadn't turned the lights on for us. A dim yellow glow lit our way.

"Hey. That guy's staring at me," Tim whispered, pointing to one of the pictures. "And so is that lady."

"I know," I answered. The pictures were even creepier in the dark.

"Let's go straight to the cemetery," Ashley said. "We have to look in that hole by the coffin." She led the way up the narrow stairs and entered the dining room.

Ashley walked around the table to the door on the left. "Uh-oh. We have a problem," she told us. "The door is locked."

"Try the door on the right," I suggested. "We can probably find another way into the cemetery from there."

Ashley nodded and opened the door.

63

"Whoa!" she said. "We've never been in here before!"

Inside was a mad scientist's laboratory. Vials of bright green, orange, and blue liquid bubbled and boiled. Lightning crackled inside a large clear ball.

The only light in the room came from the glowing vials and the lightning. Our shadows flickered on the walls.

"Hee-hee-hee-hee-heeee!" That horrible laugh was back!

"It's the ghost!" Tim shouted.

"Hee-hee-hee-hee-heeee!"

"Where is it?" I cried.

Z-zap! The room went totally dark. I heard a thump. Then silence.

"Mary-Kate—" Ashley began.

An overhead light clicked on. I could see everything in the room clearly now. Everything *except* Tim.

He was gone!

DETECTIVE TRICK

TOP TO BOTTOM CODE

Can you crack the code below? Start with the first horizontal column. Going from left to right, write down the letters that have dots next to them. Do the same for every ▶ column.

A	B	C	D	E	F	G	H	I	J	K	L	M	N	O	P	Q	R	S	T	U	V	W	X	Y	Z
		●																							
					●																				
●																									
									●																
											●														
													●												
															●										
																				●					

Did you discover the secret word? It's "carnival." Now make your own code. Start with a blank graph and fill in the dots under the letters in your secret message. Then send it to a friend!

From
The Case Of The GIGGLING GHOST

DETECTIVE TRICK

EWWW, GROSS!

In *The Case of the Giggling Ghost*, Mary-Kate and Ashley's friends think they find ghost slime called ectoplasm at the scene of each crime. Do you believe there is such a thing as ectoplasm? Ghost hunters do! Which of the following do you think they believe about ectoplasm?

1. **Yes or No:** Most ectoplasm is invisible—you can only see it in photographs.

2. **Yes or No:** Ectoplasm has magical powers. If you touch it, you'll instantly know what the ghost who left it looks like!

3. **Yes or No:** If you eat ectoplasm, you'll live forever!

4. **Yes or No:** Ectoplasm tastes just like chocolate! Mmm!

Answers:
1) Yes, 2) Yes,
3) No, 4) No

Look for our next mystery . . .
The Case Of The CANDY CANE CLUE

Boo!

"Tiiiiiim!" I cried.

No answer.

"Tim!" Ashley and Eric shouted together.

We turned and ran from the lab. Then we burst out the front door—and saw Tim standing outside waiting for us!

Ashley's blue eyes widened. "How did you get out here?" she asked.

"And why did you leave us in there?" I added.

"I didn't leave you on purpose," Tim said.

"The lights went out. And I started feeling my way around. Then *whoosh!*"

"*Whoosh?*" I repeated. "What does that mean?"

"I bumped into a section of the wall," Tim explained, "and *whoosh*, the wall flipped around. I was on the other side of it."

"That sounds kind of fun," Ashley admitted.

"And that wasn't even the best part!" Tim exclaimed. "The only way out was a Super Slide. When I got to the bottom, I was out of the house!"

"Wow. That's pretty cool," I told him.

A long, high shriek filled the evening air.

"I know that scream!" Ashley exclaimed.

"So do I," I shot back. "It's Rachel!"

Ashley, Tim, Eric, and I raced back to our booth as fast as we could. Rachel was standing on the counter. Her face was pale and her whole body was shaking.

"What happened?" Ashley asked.

"I was putting the stuffed animals under the counter of the booth," Rachel said. "Then I turned around and saw that!"

Rachel pointed to the floor of the booth. A glob of purple goo lay quivering there.

"The ghost was here!" Tim shouted.

"There is no ghost," I reminded him. But my knees trembled as I walked up to the pile of purple goo. I pulled a new container from a shelf. Then I scooped the goo inside.

"What's that?" Ashley pointed to a slip of paper on the ground.

I peered down. "It's a note," I answered. I picked it up and handed it to Ashley.

Ashley's brow creased as she read the note to herself.

"What does it say?" Rachel asked.

"It's from the Giggling Ghost," Ashley told us. "It says 'If you want me to stop haunting you, leave Patty and Eric at the coffin in my cemetery tomorrow night!'"

EATING THE EVIDENCE

"**A**re we going to give Patty and Eric to the ghost?" Rachel asked.

"Of course not," I told her.

"But the ghost is going to keep haunting us if we don't," Rachel protested.

"There isn't any ghost," Ashley said. "And Mary-Kate and I are going to prove it."

I opened my backpack and pulled out the fortune-telling card from the Giggling Ghost. Ashley and I compared the handwriting on the note to the writing on the card.

I let out a shaky breath. The handwriting matched.

"Patty could have written both," Ashley whispered to me.

"But if Patty is trying to scare Rachel, wouldn't she write a note that said we have to turn *Rachel* over to the ghost?" I whispered back. "Why would she ask for herself?"

Ashley shook her head. "This case is getting more and more confusing."

I held the plastic container full of goo close to my chest. "Well, we have one clue left," I said. "Tonight we'll examine it, and maybe we'll figure out who the ghost really is."

When we arrived home, dinner was ready, so we had to eat. *Then* we had to load the dishwasher. *Then* we had to walk our basset hound, Clue. *Then* we had to play just one game with our little sister Lizzie so she would go to bed.

"Whew!" I said once Lizzie was all tucked in.

"Now we can finally get started. Where did you put the ectoplasm sample?" Ashley asked.

"In the fridge," I told her.

"Good thinking," she said. "The cold will keep the sample in great condition."

We hurried into the kitchen. Ashley yanked open the fridge. I pulled out the first plastic container I spotted and ripped off the top.

"That's spaghetti!" Ashley exclaimed.

"Whoops! Leftovers from last night," I said. I checked the fridge again. "That's weird. I don't see it anywhere."

Ashley stuck her whole head inside the fridge. "Are you sure you put it in here?" she asked.

"Absolutely," I answered.

Ashley stepped away from the fridge. "I don't believe it. It's gone."

"We lost the ectoplasm *again*!" I cried.

"Are you girls looking for dessert, too?" our dad asked as he came into the kitchen. He dropped a plastic container in the sink.

I couldn't stop staring at the container. It was the same size as the one that I had put the ectoplasm in.

"Hey! Where did you get that?" Ashley asked.

"You didn't get it out of the fridge did you?" I asked.

"Oh, I'm sorry. Did you girls want some?" Dad gave us an apologetic smile. "I ate it all myself."

"No way!" Ashley shrieked.

"Dad," I wailed, "you *ate* our evidence!"

13

A Slimy Solution

Dad ate the only clue we had left—the slimy, shivery ectoplasm. Gross!

Dad raised his eyebrows. "You mean, that Jell-O was evidence?" he asked.

"Jell-O?" Ashley repeated.

"Yep. Grape Jell-O. And it was pretty tasty," Dad answered.

I ran over to the sink. I stared into the plastic container. A little chunk of purple goo clung to the side of it.

Slowly, I scooped up the goo. I smelled

it. Then I popped the goo into my mouth. "Dad's right. It *is* grape Jell-O," I said.

"I saw another box in the cupboard," Dad said. "Lime. Want me to make it?"

"Uh, no thanks," Ashley told him.

"I'll be in the living room if you change your minds," he said. Then he headed out of the kitchen.

I sat at the kitchen table. Ashley sat across from me. She shook her head. "I can't believe it."

"I know. The ghost slime was Jell-O all along," I said.

"We should have known that," Ashley insisted. "After all, we just had some at the class Halloween party on Thursday."

"Right," I agreed. "The Jell-O the Rachel brought."

Ashley's eyes lit up. "Mary-Kate! Where is your backpack?"

"Hanging from the hook by the door," I answered. "Why?"

"I have to check something," Ashley told me. "Do you still have the Halloween cards we got at the party?"

"Sure," I said.

"Then get ready." Ashley grinned. "Because we are about to solve this case!"

"Do you think our plan will work?" Ashley asked as we hung out at our booth on Saturday morning.

"I hope so," I answered. I tightened my grip on our dog Clue's leash. She was part of the plan.

We had gotten to the carnival an hour earlier than our friends. I had a hunch about Rachel's key chain that I needed to check out before anyone else arrived.

Now the carnival was opening and tons of people were already filing in. I guessed the OOH people outside weren't able to stop people from having fun on Halloween after all.

"Hey! Did you two solve the case yet?" Patty called as she walked up to our booth. She was with Eric, Tim, and Rachel.

Ashley and I looked at each other.

"We decided there's only one way to solve the case," I said.

"How?" Rachel asked.

"We have to bring Eric and Patty to the cemetery," I answered.

"No way!" Eric protested.

"Don't worry," Ashley said quickly. "We'll be with you the whole time. And so will Clue. She'll protect you."

"We'll all go at the end of the day," I said. Then I glanced at Ashley.

"I wish I could go, too," Rachel said. "But my mom is picking me up early today."

"Y-you're too ch-chicken to go anyway," Patty told Rachel.

But Patty and Eric didn't look too brave either. In fact, they looked downright scared. But when the carnival closed for the day, we dragged them over to the haunted house anyway.

"You know what?" Tim said as we were leaving the booth. His voice came out in a squeak. He seemed afraid, too. "I think I'll just stay here."

"Suit yourself," I said. "We'll be back in a few minutes." On the way, we passed Daisy at the information booth.

"We're taking Patty and Eric to the haunted house to meet the ghost," Ashley told her.

"Cool!" Daisy exclaimed. "Can I come with you?"

"Sure," I said.

"I'm going to see a real ghost!" Daisy exclaimed. "I'm so excited."

"Hey, Billy," Ashley called when we reached the haunted house. "Do you mind letting us in?"

Billy smiled. "Well I'm closed for the day...but I guess it's okay."

The door to the haunted house opened in front of us. We led everyone up the stairs, across the dining room, and into the cemetery.

I peered into the dimness. The graves glowed with an eerie green light. "The coffin is over there." I pointed to the left. "That's where we have to go."

I took Patty by the arm. Ashley put her hand on Eric's shoulder. We walked them over to the coffin. For a minute, everyone was silent.

"Oh, well. The ghost isn't here," Eric said. "Let's leave."

"*Hee-hee-hee-hee-heeeee! Hee-hee-hee-hee-heeeee!*" A soft giggling answered him.

Clue gave a sharp bark. A shimmery white figure rose out from behind a tombstone. It was the ghost!

"The ghost is going to get us!" Eric screamed. "Helllp!"

14

GOTCHA!

"**L**eave me alone! I'm not going with you!" Patty shouted.

The ghost giggled. Its white body fluttered as it floated closer...closer.

I let go of Clue's leash. "Now, girl!" I ordered.

Clue raced toward the ghost. She chomped down and ran back to me, holding a glittery white sheet in her teeth.

Everyone stared at the figure standing in front of us.

"Rachel!" Patty exclaimed. "I thought you went home early."

"No way!" Daisy cried. "Rachel is the ghost?"

I tossed Clue a doggie treat. "Good girl!" I cried. I scratched behind her ears.

"I can't believe *you* did this!" Eric yelled.

"Don't feel bad. We just figured it out last night," I explained.

"It started when we found out that the ectoplasm was really grape Jell-O," Ashley began.

"And we knew Rachel brought grape Jell-O to the Halloween party," I added.

"So we found a Halloween card Rachel gave us," Ashley said. "And the handwriting on the card matched the handwriting on the fortune from the Giggling Ghost!"

"Figuring out the rest was easy." I said. "On the first day of the carnival, Rachel's cousin Billy got here before we did. He put the creepy message into the fortune-telling machine."

"Then he swiped the fish and smeared the ghost slime over everything. Right, Billy?" Ashley called.

Billy stepped out from behind a tall tombstone. He held his hands above his head. "You caught me!" He smiled.

"But why did you do it, Rachel?" Eric demanded.

"You wanted to get Patty and Eric back for scaring you all the time, right?" I asked.

"Yes!" Rachel admitted. "I was tired of you making me scream. I wanted you to know how it felt to be scared."

"I wasn't scared," Eric shot back.

"Yes, you were!" Patty exclaimed. "And so was I. You really got us good, Rachel."

"Okay, so I was scared," Eric mumbled. "Especially when I heard that creepy giggling. How did you do that anyway?"

"That was the toughest part of the mystery," I admitted. "And we almost didn't figure it out."

Ashley nodded. "It's a good thing Rachel dropped that key chain the other day."

"I thought the key chain looked familiar. Then I realized that we have one almost exactly like it at home. It's a remote control for a mini tape recorder," I explained. "Whenever Rachel pushed the button on the remote, a mini tape recorder played that creepy giggling sound."

"Mary-Kate and I checked around. We found a mini recorder taped to the back of the fortune-telling machine *and* a recorder taped to Patty and Eric's booth—two of the places we heard the laughter!"

"But what about when we heard the laughing in the haunted house?" Eric asked.

"Billy played the giggling over the house's sound system," I explained.

"It's true," Billy said. "I wanted to help Rachel get back at Eric and Patty. No one gets to tease my little cousin but me."

"We just wanted to scare Patty and Eric. We didn't mean to wreck the carnival. Really!" Rachel exclaimed.

"Well, at least people showed up today," Billy said, "and we made lots of money for charity. But we're going to tell everybody the truth."

"That's great!" Ashley cheered.

"Hee-hee-hee-hee-heeeee!"

"Rachel!" Patty cried. "Stop that!"

"It-it's not me," Rachel said. "Really!"

"It's not me either," Billy said.

"Who is it then?" Patty shouted.

"It's the ghost!" Daisy cheered. "I knew it! I knew it!"

I pulled my own remote control key chain out of my pocket. I pressed the red button. Ashley held up a small recorder.

"Hee-hee-hee-hee-heee!" The sound echoed through the haunted house.

Ashley and I grinned. "Happy Halloween, everyone!"

Hi from both of us,

What could be more fun than a birthday party at the world's biggest toy store?

Ashley and I were psyched to go to our friend Patty's party at the Tower of Toys. There were tons of dolls and games to play with—and all the candy we could eat!

But then something happened that made the party not-so-fun. Want to find out what it was? Turn the page for a sneak-peek at *The New Adventures of Mary-Kate & Ashley: The Case of the Candy Cane Clue.*

See you next time!

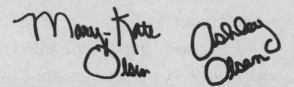

The Case Of The
CANDY CANE CLUE

When we reached the top floor Candy led us to the back of the store. I saw a red neon sign flashing TOY OF THE YEAR!

Underneath the sign was a glass case on a platform. Inside was a feathery green doll with long arms and legs and big eyeballs.

The doll's head tilted from side to side as he began to sing: "Let it snow! Let it snow! Let it snooooow!"

"That's Sing-along Sammy!" Ashley cried.

"Sammy is so cool!" I took a step closer to the glass case.

An ear-splitting alarm filled the store. It was followed by a voice that boomed over a loudspeaker: "STAND BACK!"

"Okay, okay!" I quickly jumped back.

"What's the big deal?" Patty scoffed. "It's not like he's the last Sammy on earth."

Candy gave us a serious look. "Actually, he is," she said.

"No way!" Patty gasped. "I want the last Sammy on earth."

Candy shook her head. "Sorry. The last Sammy is not for sale. He's for display only."

The soldiers guarding snapped back into position in front of Sammy the toy.

"Come on," Candy said. "Let's check out all the toys and games you *can* play with!"

We headed back downstairs.

"Oh, no! I left my bucket of candy next to the Sammy display!" Patty whined.

"Ashley and I will get it, Patty," I said.

We headed back to the Toy of the Year display. But when we got there something was terribly wrong.

The toy soldiers were gone.

And so was Sammy!

WIN A MARY-KATE AND ASHLEY
Best Friends Prize Pack!

WIN <u>TWO</u> OF EACH OF THE FABULOUS PRIZES LISTED BELOW:
One set for you, one set for your best buddy! It's twice as nice to share the prizes!

- Autographed photo of Mary-Kate and Ashley
- A complete library of TWO OF A KIND™, THE NEW ADVENTURES OF MARY-KATE AND ASHLEY™, MARY-KATE AND ASHLEY STARRING IN, SO LITTLE TIME and SWEET 16 book series
- Mary-Kate and Ashley videos
- Mary-Kate and Ashley music CDs
- 3 sets of Mary-Kate and Ashley dolls
- Mary-Kate and Ashley video games
- Mary-Kate and Ashley Fantasy Pack

IT COULD BE YOU!

Mail to: **THE NEW ADVENTURES OF MARY-KATE AND ASHLEY**
BEST FRIENDS PRIZE PACK SWEEPSTAKES
C/O HarperEntertainment
Attention: Children's Marketing Department
10 East 53rd Street, New York, NY 10022

No purchase necessary.

Name: _____

Address: _____

City: _____ State: _____ Zip: _____

Phone: _____ Age: _____

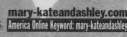

HarperEntertainment
An Imprint of HarperCollinsPublishers
www.harpercollins.com

Books from Real Girls

America Online

mary-kateandashley.com
America Online Keyword: mary-kateandashley

PARACHUTE PRESS

DUALSTAR PUBLICATIONS

OFFICIAL RULES:

1. No purchase necessary.

2. To enter complete the official entry form or hand print your name, address, age, and phone number along with the words "THE NEW ADVENTURES OF MARY-KATE & ASHLEY Win a Best Friends Prize Pack Sweepstakes" on a 3" x 5" card and mail to: THE NEW ADVENTURES OF MARY-KATE & ASHLEY Win a Best Friends Prize Pack Sweepstakes, c/o HarperEntertainment, Attn: Children's Marketing Department, 10 East 53rd Street, New York, NY 10022. Entries must be received no later than December 31, 2002. Enter as often as you wish, but each entry must be mailed separately. One entry per envelope. Partially completed, illegible, or mechanically reproduced entries will not be accepted. Sponsors are not responsible for lost, late, mutilated, illegible, stolen, postage due, incomplete, or misdirected entries. All entries become the property of Dualstar Entertainment Group, Inc., and will not be returned.

3. Sweepstakes open to all legal residents of the United States (excluding Colorado and Rhode Island) who are between the ages of five and fifteen on December 31, 2002, excluding employees and immediate family members of HarperCollins Publishers, Inc. ("HarperCollins"), Parachute Properties and Parachute Press, Inc., and their respective subsidiaries and affiliates, officers, directors, shareholders, employees, agents, attorneys, and other representatives (individually and collectively "Parachute"), Dualstar Entertainment Group, Inc., and its subsidiaries and affiliates, officers, directors, shareholders, employees, agents, attorneys, and other representatives (individually and collectively "Dualstar"), and their respective parent companies, affiliates, subsidiaries, advertising, promotion and fulfillment agencies, and the persons with whom each of the above are domiciled. Offer void where prohibited or restricted by law.

4. Odds of winning depend on the total number of entries received. Approximately 600,000 sweepstakes announcements published. All prizes will be awarded. Winner will be randomly drawn on or about January 15, 2003, by HarperEntertainment, whose decisions are final. Potential winner will be notified by mail and will be required to sign and return an affidavit of eligibility and release of liability within 14 days of notification. Prizes won by minors will be awarded to parent or legal guardian who must sign and return all required legal documents. By acceptance of prize, winner consents to the use of his or her name, photograph, likeness, and personal information by HarperCollins, Parachute, Dualstar, and for publicity purposes without further compensation except where prohibited.

5. One (1) Grand Prize Winner will win a Best Friends Prize Pack to include 2 of each of the following items: autographed photo of Mary-Kate and Ashley, THE NEW ADVENTURES OF MARY-KATE & ASHLEY book library, TWO OF A KIND book library, STARRING IN... book library, SO LITTLE TIME book library, SWEET 16 book library; MARY-KATE AND ASHLEY Fantasy Pack; MARY-KATE AND ASHLEY GIRLS' NIGHT OUT, CRUSH COURSE, POCKET PLANNER, MAGICAL MYSTERY MALL, WINNERS CIRCLE, and GET A CLUE video games; PASSPORT TO PARIS, BILLBOARD DAD, SWITCHING GOALS, YOU'RE INVITED TO MARY-KATE AND ASHLEY'S GREATEST PARTIES, YOU'RE INVITED TO MARY-KATE AND ASHLEY'S BALLET PARTY, and YOU'RE INVITED TO MARY-KATE AND ASHLEY'S SCHOOL DANCE PARTY videos; SO LITTLE TIME Mary-Kate doll, SO LITTLE TIME Ashley doll, SWEET 16 doll car, WINNING LONDON doll giftset; HOLIDAY IN THE SUN, WINNING LONDON, OUR LIPS ARE SEALED, MARY-KATE AND ASHLEY GREATEST HITS, and MARY-KATE AND ASHLEY GREATEST HITS II music CDs. Approximate retail value: $1,500.00.

6. Only one prize will be awarded per individual, family, or household. Prize is non-transferable and cannot be sold or redeemed for cash. No cash substitute is available. Any federal, state, or local taxes are the responsibility of the winner. Sponsor may substitute prize of equal or greater value, if necessary, due to availability.

7. Additional terms: By participating, entrants agree a) to the official rules and decisions of the judges, which will be final in all respects; and to waive any claim to ambiguity of the official rules and b) to release, discharge, and hold harmless HarperCollins, Parachute, Dualstar, and their affiliates, subsidiaries, and advertising and promotion agencies from and against any and all liability or damages associated with acceptance, use, or misuse of any prize received in this sweepstakes.

8. Any dispute arising from this Sweepstakes will be determined according to the laws of the State of New York, without reference to its conflict of law principles, and the entrants consent to the personal jurisdiction of the State and Federal courts located in New York County and agree that such courts have exclusive jurisdiction over all such disputes.

9. To obtain the name of the winner, please send your request and a self-addressed stamped envelope (excluding residents of Vermont and Washington) to THE NEW ADVENTURES OF MARY-KATE & ASHLEY Win a Best Friends Prize Pack Sweepstakes, c/o HarperEntertainment, Attn: Children's Marketing Department, 10 East 53rd Street, New York, NY 10022 by February 1, 2003. Sweepstakes Sponsor: HarperCollins Publishers, Inc.

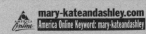